IN THE NAME OF
THE FATHER

(AND OF THE SON)

IN THE NAME OF THE FATHER

THE FATHER

(AND OF THE SON)

Immanuel Mifsud

Translated from the Maltese
by Albert Gatt

Parthian, Cardigan SA43 1ED
www.parthianbooks.com
First published in Maltese in
© Immanuel Mifsud 2019
© This translation by Albert Gatt 2019
ISBN 978-1-912681-30-3
Editor: Edward Matthews
Cover design: Syncopated Pandemonium
Typeset by Elaine Sharples
Printed by 4edge
Published with the financial support of the Books Council of Wales
British Library Cataloguing in Publication Data
A cataloguing record for this book is available from the British Library

for my brothers and sisters. Silvio, Violet, Victor, Connie, Francis, Carmen and Joe

PARTHIAN

CYNGOR LLYFRAU CYMRU
BOOKS COUNCIL of WALES

BRITISH | Wales
COUNCIL | Cymru

Co-funded by the
European Union

Creative
Europe
MEDIA

Co-funded by the Creative Europe Programme of
the European Union

Published with the financial support of
the Books Council of Wales

Immanuel Mifsud was born in Malta in 1967, the youngest in a working-class family of eight children. He has been active on the literary scene since the age of sixteen, when he started writing poetry and co-founded the literary group Versarti. He later founded several drama groups and also directed plays written by himself and by a variety of famous playwrights. He is a leading contemporary poet and fiction writer and some of his works have been translated and published in some European countries and the USA. His 2002 short story collection *L-Istejjer Strambi ta' Sara Sue Sammut* (Sara Sue Sammut's Strange Stories) won the Malta National Literary award and the same book was later nominated for the Premio Strega Europa prize. He has participated in prestigious literary festivals across Europe. Mifsud is a lecturer at the University of Malta, where he teaches modern Maltese poetry and theatre.

Albert Gatt trained as a computational linguist and is currently the Director of the Institute of Linguistics and Language Technology at the University of Malta. His research focusses on the use of language in artificial (AI) systems, particularly on the production of language from non-linguistic data, including perceptual data from computer vision. In addition to his academic research, he has been translating poetry and prose from Maltese into English for several years. Recent translations include Adrian Grima's poetry collection *Last-Ditch Ecstasy* (Malta: Midsea Books, 2017 and Mumbai: Paperwall Publishing). He has recently completed a translation of Juann Mamo's modernist classic *Nanna's Children in America* (1934).

TRANSLATOR'S NOTE

In dealing with citations, I have followed the author's own practice and used footnotes that reference the original, untranslated version of a work. Apart from direct quotations of works originally published in English, the original also contains several intertextual allusions. Here, in addition to consulting the original where this was accessible to me, I have benefited from existing translations. In particular, I would like to acknowledge the following:

Roland Barthes (1994). *Camera Lucida: Reflections on Photography*. (Richard Howard, trans.) New York: Farrar, Strauss and Giroux

Julia Kristeva (1987). *Tales of Love*. (Leon S. Roudiez, trans.) New York: Columbia University Press

Peter Handke (1974). *A Sorrow Beyond Dreams*. Ralph Mannheim, trans. London: Pushkin Press.

The lyrics of the song *Lili Marlene* are from the English version by Tommie Connor (1944).

The notes at the end of the book give some background information related to traditions, places and historical figures, which may be of help to the non-Maltese reader.

a.g.

One can confess all one wants, the unconfessable remains unconfessed.
Hélène Cixous, 'Literature Suspends Death'

Foreword

Three years before he was knocked down by a passing van, Roland Barthes was knocked back by the death of the woman with whom he had spent his whole life, his mother Henriette Barthes. The second half of *Camera Lucida*, the last work he published in his lifetime, contains some of the most moving passages he had ever written, full of feeling for this woman, probably the only one he had ever loved. Barthes says that as he studied photographs of his mother, he was merely contemplating them without really 'engulfing himself' in them; he adds that as he looked at these photographs he realised that should he ever show them to others, these images would probably not 'speak'.

A few years before my father died, while I was moving house, I discovered quite by chance a little notebook with a thick brown cover that contained a short diary that he had begun in 1939, after joining the King's Own Malta Regiment. I was aware of my father's tendency to document his personal experiences in the form of diaries; for example, in a diary written during a trip to Italy he made with one of my brothers in 1982, he recorded everything in the minutest detail, including what he ate every day and how much each taxi and train journey had cost. Although I refer to the contents of the brown notebook as a 'war diary', it really isn't such a detailed account and, when compared with works such as Ellul Mercer's *Taht in-Nar* ('Under Fire'), it contains little in the way of historically relevant information. It is in fact a rather disjointed document written by a nineteen-year-old who couldn't write very well, full of the enthusiasm and excitement brought on by the putting on of a uniform and by the dramatic events that were unfolding. As I recall, I kept the diary and decided that I would publish it in some shape or form 'when the time was ripe'.

The evening following my father's funeral, as I rocked my son – then still a babe in arms – to sleep, I picked up the brown notebook once more. Instead of the text in the diary, I found myself reading another text, one that began to surface gradually through those pages, a text composed not just of memories, but also of reflections on masculinity and fatherhood.

Like Barthes, I am a little concerned that this particular photograph won't 'speak'; for one thing, these images are formulated in a very different register from the one I am used to. But I wanted to keep my promise. I wanted to keep *this* promise to make up for so many others that I had made but never kept.

The first time I saw you cry

At the Addolorata cemetery. On your mother's grave. From behind the thick, dark lenses of your glasses, I saw the tear trickling down. It shouldn't have done that, but it did; it just welled up and trickled down. You thought I hadn't noticed anything, but I was watching you. I was always watching you, always keeping an eye on you, to see how you'd behave. Like the time I caught you with your hand behind your back, making the sign of the horns when someone remarked that you looked really well, God bless you, in spite of your age, in spite of the permanent damage to your left leg, in spite of everything you'd been through. I was always on the lookout where you were concerned. And on that day, I was watching as this tear trickled down, full of shame, the shame you would feel on another occasion when I drew your attention to another tear trickling down your cheek. On that particular day, I made you feel even more ashamed when, clinging to your wife's apron reeking of garlic and onions, I announced to all that I'd just seen you cry.

I didn't know that even soldiers cried.

I thought that soldiers were made of steel.

I thought their face was always stern and strong and tough.

I thought it was just me who cried, just me who did things I wasn't supposed to do.

Just like that day.

That day.

That was the time you used to tell me that I couldn't cry. I'm a big boy. You can't grow up and become a man if you cry. How can a boy like you still cry? How can you still cry when you're strong enough to tear this place apart? You can't cry, do you understand? You just can't.

But I do cry. And I feel ashamed when I cry. And I feel ashamed because I shouldn't cry. And I feel even more ashamed because – do you really want to hear this? – I actually like crying. I like to feel that trickle of warm water. I like the constricted sensation in my nose, my eyes screwed shut. I like it when my vision is blurred.

I like disobeying you.

I like being afraid of you because you're scary. Because you look at me and your withering look scares me. And I cower and move away.

You cry too.

Soldier, you cry too.

Just as you did on that day, when the man at your side died. Didn't you cry on that day, when you saw him get hit? Didn't you?

Just as you did on that day, when everything was pulverised before your eyes.

Just as you do whenever you remember that your wedding ceremony was held in a bomb shelter.

Underneath the lantern
By the barrack gate,
Darling I remember
The way you used to wait.
'Twas there that you whispered tenderly
That you loved me;
You'd always be
My Lili of the lamplight,
Wie einst Lili Marlene,
Wie einst Lili Marlene,

The cigarette hanging lazily from the corner of your mouth. Your hat tilted over one eye. Humphrey Bogart. Casablanca. Tripoli. Benghazi.

The stiff-collared shirt. The small, tight knot of your tie. That look. That thin moustache on a smooth face, the smell of shaving cream every morning before sunrise. Which is why, when I see the tear that I wasn't supposed to see, there by the family grave, I am stunned.

Wie einst Lili Marlene, Wie einst Lili Marlene.

I, Ġużeppi Marija Mifsud from Valletta, son of Pawla and Salvu, proletarian and committed Socialist although I have never read the red books (because those are blacklisted by our Mother the Apostolic Roman Catholic Church and because I don't have a head for difficult, evil books, though I do know how to read a little), soldier of the Second World War assigned to the anti-aircraft cannon to defend my homeland from the air assaults of the fascist Italian bastards and the Nazi pigs, risking my life for my homeland, for the family entrusted to my care by the grace of God, with tattoos on my arm because I'm a proletarian soldier – a corporal at first, then a sergeant in the King's Own Malta Regiment and the Royal Malta Artillery in Bigi and Tignè – my skin blistered by white-hot steel, toiling as I had always done since childhood after my mother was widowed for the second time, running about the streets wearing only one shoe in order to make the pair last longer, taking on whatever jobs I could find to support my mother and my younger siblings and learning the facts of life on street corners, rinsing spittle, sauce and fried egg yolk off plates and glasses in village bars, checking passenger tickets on the bus, bending double in the factories in Marsa and getting covered with soot and coal fragments, becoming a man as men are supposed to be, a hymn to barefooted humanity and an inspiration for the Workers' Movement, living and dying and taking aim at the enemy flying overhead in aeroplanes intent on blowing my head off, becoming, existing, being.

At the age of forty-seven, I welcomed my eighth child with open arms; he would have been the tenth had all my children survived. And I said to the Lord: Lord, thy will be done, for even though I thought I'd finally earned a rest, having brought up a family and defended my homeland and the One True Faith, thy Providence looked down upon me from on high and recognised my abilities and saw that I still had the necessary strength in spite of all that had happened to me, all I had been through, all I had witnessed and thereby sent me another child. I do not know how I will support this added burden that came so unexpectedly, but I place my trust in thee, O Lord, as I have always done.

At the age of eighty-seven, Lord, you summoned me unto you.

Ġużeppi Marija Mifsud, also known as *il-Kikkra*, The Cup.

Now, son let's see if you can guess this one: from her lips a kiss you stole, with your finger in her hole.

Go on then, what is it?

And I blush: my mind has been sullied already and I suspect you've noticed and you're trying to see just how dirty-minded I've become. *Go on, what is it? From her lips a kiss you stole, with your finger in her hole.* And I remain silent because I'm not sure what you expect: whether you're trying to see how much of a man I've become or whether I remain the little boy I've always been. And then you smile and say: *It's a cup, thicko!* Oh right, a cup. And there I was, wandering through the grimy alleyways of my mind that rather resemble the streets you used to run about in half-shod, thinking that you might perhaps be talking about this girl I was with last night when I was supposed to be at the mass for the First Friday of the month. The Cup – that's your nickname, isn't it? Mifsud, *il-Kikkra*.

Those heavy, black boots. Mismatched. These boots are meant to conceal your handicap. Somewhere on the way to Madliena, a soldier riding a motorbike up the hill. Somewhere in Madliena, a soldier lying unconscious in a field. One year in the military hospital at Bigi. Another year in the military hospital in London.

When you get home you collapse onto the nearest chair and unlace your boots. You always unlace the left boot first. And you ask me to pull your boots off for you. Once they're off, they feel heavy in my hands. And you tell me to line them up neatly under the bed. And you roll along like a boat on a rough sea. And the sea gets rougher once your boots are off. No shortness of breath, in spite of all the cigarettes you smoke; you're able to dive to the very bottom of the bay below Xgħajra Tower to bring up sea urchins. Scores of sea urchins in the wicker basket. They reek of the sea. The smell of sea urchins is alien to me and I've never been down to Xgħajra Tower and those dark depths scare me. I'm afraid. I'm afraid of a lot of things: of the cemetery you take me to every other Sunday; of the big horses belonging to the mounted police that you take me to see; of your left leg, twisted out of all proportion; of dogs; of the grasshoppers that leap among the hundred-leaved roses in the corner of our yard; of the tortoise you smuggled in without a permit, hidden in the rucksack you used to carry en route to Tripoli, to Benghazi; of the litter of cats that jump about and multiply and give birth in the wardrobes in Leli Cousin's house next door; of Leli Cousin himself, reeking of sweat, piss and *Du Maurier* cigarettes; of the darkness that falls every evening; of thunder; of lightning; of the earth's tremors one night in 1972; of the high blood pressure you suffer from; of your voice raised in anger; of the belt you begin to undo whenever I disobey you; of the glasses across your face; of your pointed moustache; of the green tattoos on your arm; of your age; of the death which I fear will take my mother away from me at any moment; of the disfigured face of Christ on the cross; of the photograph of your mother with her slack bottom lip; of all the mysterious stories of my aunt Stella, whom I've never seen but whom I'd really like to meet some day; of the thieves who broke into Rexie's place and made off with fifty quid after giving her a beating and throttling her; of the ghosts you claim you used to see in the tenement building in Valletta where your aunt Basilica used to live; of the Socialist stalwarts who would troop past our place escorting minister Lorry or minister Grima; of the vindictive state apparatus that transferred you to a different post at work because you couldn't keep your trap shut and spoke your mind; of the dream I used to dream every night of a moribund man whom I watched as he lay dying, a doll falling out from under his bed just as he breathed his last; of the shadow that doggedly pursued me (that's what you used to tell me: *You're afraid of your own shadow!*); and above all: of you.

You filled my dreams with a heavy military tread; with the crackle of Bofors guns; the screech of Stukas diving out of the sky. You filled my dreams with regurgitated Fasces and the English officers who took the piss out of you, this little Maltese man who chewed on husks of bread and nibbled at hard white cheese and brought children into the world. And I asked you so many times: *What's that Cross doing on our flag?* And you would promptly take out your photographs, show off the scar in your left thigh and tell me the stories that had swollen in the damp of the bomb shelter where your wedding ceremony was held in February 1942. You filled my dreams with barrel-chested heroes baring their chests and standing chest out to defend their homeland, to defend the British Crown which shone brightly over this island. You filled my childhood with the sound of Dame Vera Lynn, *We'll meet again, don't know where, don't know when; but I'm sure we'll meet again some sunny day.*

> *On the 21st Dec 1939 I joined the British army and was enlisted in the 2nd Battalion. The King's Own Malta Regiment, this Regiment was stationed at St.Andrews barracks and we were instructed by the NCO's of differenti units. The first day that I spent at the barracks I was very happy, my comrades used to teach me how I must fowled the blankits and how to mount the equipment how to clean the Rifle.*

I found your diary, bound in dark brown, and nicked it. And I kept it. *On the 21st Dec 1939 I joined the British army and was enlisted in the 2nd Battalion.* At the age of nineteen they handed you a rifle with a bayonet and dressed you up in a uniform and took you to St Andrew's to learn how to shoot.

The following day I was marched to the Quarter Master store to collect the rest of my uniform after I had all my uniform I was told by the company sargeant major to take off my Plain clothes and to put on the uniform so I did as I was told. I put the army boots and socks and then I put on the overall dress and the equipment and a stif cap I tooked the Rifle and went the first time on parade I was placed at No 9 Squad under the Instructor L/c Homes of Royal Irish. The Instructor after he spoke to me and recognised that speaks english he told that I will be squad leader. From now on I started the army life.

And so you took your vow of loyalty to the Crown and of all your vows, you kept this one right till the end. According to Jessica Meyer, in Britain at the turn of the twentieth century, the soldier was held up as the epitome of the imperial ideal and of true masculinity.[1] You had to have guts in order to be a soldier, and men had to show that they had something down there, otherwise they'd be considered boys, little more than adolescents. You were a man. The diaries the soldiers kept during wartime, Meyer continues, demonstrate their attempt to document the experiences that they used to live through, from everyday activities such as cooking and washing up, to commentaries about the weather, the fear of bombing raids and the battles. In her study of a large number of soldiers' diaries Meyer observes that, unlike the letters they sent to their families, home hardly ever featured in these soldiers' diaries.[2]

At the age of nineteen they handed you a rifle with a bayonet and dressed you up in a uniform and took you to St Andrew's to learn how to shoot and somehow, you managed to get your hands on a little, dark brown notebook and a pen. You wanted to write. You wanted to write your story so that someday your son would write the story of your story.

---

[1] Meyer, Jessica (2009) *Men of War: Masculinity and the First World War in Britain*, Hampshire: Palgrave Macmillan, 5

[2] Meyer, 48

At the age of nineteen, I was studying. At the age of nineteen, I was no longer afraid: I'd left my shadow behind me and I dreamt of the revolution that would follow on the heels of civil disobedience and passive resistance. By then I was used to disobedience and I'd mastered a form of resistance to the power of the King. Perhaps you were right: destiny does hold us under its sway, as you believed. Or perhaps I am what I am simply because I was cast in your mould. At the age of nineteen – actually, well before then – I had committed my umpteenth betrayal. The first person I betrayed was you.

For at the window of my house, I looked through my casement and I discerned among the youth a young man void of understanding, passing through the street near the corner where a certain woman lived. In the black and dark night, he went the way to her house. And there met him a woman with the attire of a harlot and subtle of heart. Face to face, they looked at each other. In her frenzy and disquietude, she abides not in her house, this woman, but roams the streets, or lies in wait, now at the end of the street, now in the square, now at street corners. So she caught him and kissed him and looking straight into his eyes, said unto him: 'This day I have paid my vows. Therefore I came forth to seek you, to meet you, to find you. And here you are. I have decked my bed with coverings of tapestry and perfumed my sheets with myrrh, aloes, and cinnamon. Come, let us take our fill of love until the morning, for my husband is not at home – he is gone on a long journey. He has taken a bag of money with him and will not come home before the full moon.' She drew him to her, she enchanted him, with her fair speech she caused him to yield. And, fool that he is, he goes after her straightaway, as an ox goes to the slaughter, as a deer is tied to the stocks until a dart strike through his liver, as a bird hastens unwittingly to the snare. Listen to me now, therefore, my son, and attend to my words. Let not your heart decline to her ways. Go not astray in her paths. For she has cast down many wounded. The path to her house will lead you to drowning, it leads to the chambers of death.

But I did not attend to your words. That was the germ of my rebellion.

You filled my dreams with the bare footfalls of a young boy, limping along with one shoe on, the other sole covered in sores. Limping along. Limping down a street littered with animal droppings. You filled my dreams with Socialism, with its loves and hatreds. Hey, you, you Socialist who rises each day professing loyalty to the workers: you who lambasted the meek workers who sought to have their daily bread without having their picture stamped on a Party membership card. Hey, you!

The ?? used to sound at 0630 and we used to get up the bed and go to wash and some of the soldiers use to shave, after we put the bed properly and the Bugle sound for PT this is the first parade during the day after the first parade is over we go in the barrack room and dress and we parade again for breakfast. After breakfast we used to go to dress for the drill we polish the boots clean the bads put the equipment on get the rifle and will be ready outside the room to be fall in. At 0830hrs we fall in the Instructor makes the roll to see if any body is missing and then we march to the parade ground, at the parade an inspection will perform by the Officer in charge and the Instructor to see if every body is clean. After the inspection we carry on with the program.

The stains of engine oil and gunpowder make your hands smell even better. Your hands are fearless, unhesitating; nothing repels them. Your hands expect to stain with blood, some day. So when they feel the rifle for the first time, when they grasp it tightly, the fingers curling round, embracing, it is as though they heave a sigh, of one who has finally arrived. As does the rest of you, ensconced in a uniform the colour of desert storms. You wait for the right moment. You raise the rifle, shut one eye and take aim. In silence. Perfectly calm and collected. You pull the trigger and your chest is shattered by the recoil from the bullet's flight. The tremors from that shot have quaked your chest. It's nearly thrown you back. But you are solid, strong and sinewy, your veins flow with tongues of fire. You stand your ground, reload in time to close one eye, take your aim upon the order and FIRE! You fire.

You're there in every film I watch about soldiers. I watch them tell the same stories you tell. I watch them: their stance, their look, everything is just the same. These are real men, not adolescents.

1983. September. *The Wall* at the Upper Savoy cinema. Alone in the theatre, I watch your story unfold once more. I look at the little boy with his father's uniform. Eric Fletcher Waters fought in the same war as you, under the same Crown, against the same demons. Eric Fletcher Waters. The name has such a nice ring to it. Maybe it's because it's an English name. Maybe it's because it's the name of a hero. As for you, somehow, a name like Ġużeppi Marija Mifsud suits you better. Ġużeppi Marija Mifsud, bombardier, corporal, army sergeant. There's this aeroplane screeching across the sky aiming bullets at an A/A battery and there's Eric Fletcher Waters desperately calling on the telephone. There's the telephone receiver dangling and Eric Fletcher Waters lying prone, eyes wide open, face drenched with blood, breathless, lifeless. There's this Stuka screeching across the sky, loud and persistent. Not just one. They're swarming. And the A/A on the Bofors firing for all they're worth. You're there among them, Ġużeppi Marija Mifsud, number 11408, RC (*Roman Catholic*) so that, should you end up like Eric Fletcher Waters, they'll know what last rites suit you best. The dog tags around your neck bear the legend: 11408 Joseph Mary Mifsud, RC.

I got to watch your film too. On a sheet that was never unfurled. I watched it in the stories that you told me in those afternoons, lounging on the big bed at the end of Laurel and Hardy films, or as we drove back home in the Cortina with the rays of sunlight floating in my hair streaked with salt from the bay at Birżebbuġa. I watched your film in those pages that smelt of soldiers, scrawled with your unmistakeable handwriting in black ink that's gone brown with age. I watched your film in photographs of soldiers smiling and exhausted, or standing straight as their rifles somewhere in Pembroke or Hal Far.

On the 11th June 1940 Italy declared War against the allies, and the next morning 25 Aircraft were over the island and bomd it for 11 times during the day, a terrible panic was all over the island special at the three cities.

The soldiers were told to not leave their post until further orders and were stayed at the Fort for 2 months. After Italy declared War 'Conscription started in Malta'.

In November 1940 I was shifted to Busketto Garden for a ?? course and during the course I was made up War Substantive Corporal, after the course I went to Rabat Station.

1941

In the year 1941 I went to St Andrew's to teach the conscripts recruits and in the same year the Battalion became in a Static Group under the Command of Major Mallia.

In the year 1941 in January the Nazi airforce joined the Italian airforce combined where over the island and we and the civilian population were in a great danger. In Oct of the same year at about 0200 2 ME planes attacked a Gozo boat and some of the passengers were killed some of the soldiers went down into the sea to give help. After we finished from the recruiting training we went back to our corps.

Alone in the theatre at the Upper Savoy, my tears well up: a trickle at first, then a deluge. With my cigarette burnt into a long column of ash, I look at the black and white images unfurling on the sheet, images of soldiers and aeroplanes screeching incessantly, diving as low as possible to sow seeds of steel that shatter everything in sight. These are the same stories you told me in our back yard as you carved lanterns for me out of watermelon skins or peeled prickly pears or gnawed at frozen Coca Cola or Ovaltine cubes.

Wie einst Lili Marlene.
Wie einst Lili Marlene.

Lili Marlene wasn't exactly blonde and she never waited for you underneath the lantern. She'd probably never ventured across her mother's doorstep. She was a refugee from Bormla sharing a house in Qormi with people she didn't know from Adam. According to Lili Marlene, they'd gather around the dining table and, since there wasn't enough cutlery and crockery to go round, they'd all plunge their hands into a large pot to eat. But then, one fine day, you spotted her and fixed her with your gaze. Although you never told me the story in full, I could swear she must have blushed and lowered her eyes and rushed back indoors. In February 1942 you took her for your wife. True to your upbringing in the streets, you didn't give a toss for regiment protocol and got married in civvies, so that you had to keep your wedding photographs concealed for a long time afterwards. She'd had her wedding dress made by a dressmaker in Mdina, had Lili Marlene, and she'd walk all the way up there to have her measurements taken and one day she got the fright of her life when an air raid was launched while she was on the way up. Afterwards, you went down into the shelter in Qormi to eat your *biskuttin*. Lili Marlene slept deeply that night; she had no clue about the nocturnal rituals of marriage. She was nineteen and she'd always lived in her mother's shadow. Many years later, while you were picking my brains to see if I'd learned how babies get made, you told me the story of Lili Marlene and the first night you spent with her with the priest's blessing. *The next day, her pa turned up and asked me how things had gone. And I said: I could give her back to you intact. And Nannu went up to Nanna and said: Marija, didn't you ever have a chat with our daughter? And Nanna took your mother aside and had a chat with her. And that evening, your mother cried her eyes out and asked me why I hadn't told her what she was supposed to do.*

Lili Marlene, sive Vincenza Mifsud née Delezio, kept on doing as she was told until the day she died in her sleep. That's how she'd been brought up by her mother and taught by you. As I rifled through the little dark brown notebook I came across your little philosophical treatise, divided into two parts:

> *Man should have 3 Hearts. A heart of flame burning with love for God another of flesh beating with love for his neighbour and Another of Bronze to repress the desires of the Body; and the Family has to be under The Rule of the Father; If the man is a chicken and the Wife is a Cock, then the whole Family is turned Upside Dawn.*

You were the head of the family, the top dog, the chief, the almighty, the man, the potent phallus before whom everyone bowed. In spite of your diminutive height. In spite of the handicap that made you even shorter. You were a War veteran, decorated with medals that Britannia had pinned to your chest in recognition of your service, your loyalty and above all, your courage during the siege.

Me, I was the thorn in your side.

I was the thorn in your side with which you were well pleased, even though it pricked you.

In the theatre, the house lights dim and there is silence. Darkness. The curtains go up. A house in the country. I'm sitting there awaiting catharsis. There's this moustachioed man with a piercing stare, a cape draped over his arm, a cane in his right hand. He stops and stands in the middle.

> *Madamigella Valery?*
> *Son io.*

D'Alfredo il padre in me vedete!
Voi!
Sì, dell'incauto, che a ruina corre, ammaliato da voi.

Ritorna di tuo padre orgoglio e vanto.
Be once again your father's pride and joy.

In the name of the father

Susan Bordo opens her book *The Male Body*[3] with her memories of her father, who learnt the ways of the world from the streets, just like you. Like you, he was the father, the Father, THE father. In Brooklyn, Mr Bordo skived and connived with his street fellows, with the Jewish mafia; later, he would tell his stories to his two children. He was the macho type, was Mr Bordo – just like you. Except that he smoked cigars, rather than a hundred cigarettes a day, and he went around in a three-piece suit and a fedora. You too had a picture of yourself in a three-piece, hat tilted over one eye, cigarette in the corner of your mouth. You wanted to emulate the Hollywood greats: Humphrey Bogart with his heavy stare holding a cigarette, a shot glass in the other hand. The last time Bordo saw her father, he was old and frail, and seemed to her to have become like a little boy, delicate and fragile.

My relatives had warned me, as I got ready to drive down for what I knew would be a final visit, that his appearance might be shocking and upsetting to me. What I was not prepared for was the deep comfort – perhaps it could even be called pleasure – that I got from simply being alone with him, close to his body, from holding his hand or touching his shoulder as long as I wanted to, from looking at him with such an unobstructed intimacy of gaze, from lingering with him and over him. Exhausted, cocooned in a state of consciousness that was neither sleep nor waking, he mostly merely lay there, accepting my physical closeness, my

---

[3] Bordo, Susan (1999) *The Male Body: a New Look at Men in Public and in Private*, New York: Farrar, Straus and Giroux

caresses. Just once, he spoke to me. He told me he was cold, and he asked
me to cover him. When I did, he thanked me with the grace of a courtier,
[...]: 'Thank you, doll. Thank you, doll.' As wretched as he looked, I
feasted on the sight of him as if he were my infant boy, and it was very
hard to leave his side. [4]

These moments keep coming back to me, these digital pictures, these
3D after-images, of the soldier gradually approaching the end of the
battle. In spite of the siege that you came through unscathed, the
aeroplanes you shot down, the handicap that became both a bane and
something of a joke, you were destined to lose the final battle.
Naturally. Just like the soldiers that had come before and would come
after you. And yet there are also images from an earlier time when the
soldier still stood tall, or rather, from a time when the soldier simply
refused to be told.

Discipline and order. Those were the twin tracks along which you
moved.

But towards the end of the seventies, thinking that Bogart could
get one up on a Socialist minister, you let your tongue wag a little too
much and found yourself in fucking deep shit, Mifsud. What was that
all about, all that talk against the government and the minister for
public works, a fellow who'd been your eldest son's schoolmate, mind
you? Who the fuck did you think you were to talk like that against the
Workers' government? A little nobody, a watchman, lame like the devil
himself. Who the hell did you think you were? Well then, as from
tomorrow morning, you will kindly report to work on the other side
of the island, handicap, old age and all. That'll teach you to keep your
gob shut, idiot. You can take all your medals, all your health conditions
and stuff the lot.

And you get home from work. You say nothing. And you lean your
rifle with the chipped bayonet against the wall. And quietly, timidly,

---

[4] Bordo, 11

you limp to your corner. You can't bite the hand that feeds you, didn't you learn that lesson from the streets? It doesn't take a genius to work out that the Worker's government is untouchable, does it? That the minister is the Lord thy god and thou shalt have no gods before him. And above all, that thou shalt not take the holy name of the minister in vain? That day, you seemed so quiet, without your glasses, lying down on your side like a wounded man, cursing the day that you didn't take us all on board that ship to sail to the other end of the earth. Cursing the day you proudly proclaimed that you too were a proletarian, wearing only one shoe. They told you that you were a hero, the proletarian aristocrat, the apple in the eye of the revolutionary class, and you believed them. They told you that all animals are equal, even the pigs, and you believed them. But they never mentioned that some are more equal than others.

And only then, during that melancholy afternoon, did I finally get the answer to the question I had asked you so many times and which you always refused to answer: we were not 'with Mintoff'. I'd had my doubts in any case, because during the election campaign of 1976 the kids in our street and at school would all proclaim that they were with Mintoff and with Lorry Sant and with Moran and with Grima, while I would keep quiet, having no idea who these illustrious gentlemen were. And when I got home and asked you, you said: 'I won't have any talk of politics.' And then you added, as you always did: 'You're far too young for that.' But I always heard you talk of 'us' and 'them' and 'our lot' and 'the others'. And during the eight o'clock news I had to be all tiptoes and whispers. And you'd listen to the political debates on the Philips television set that could only tune in to TVM and Rai Uno, you'd listen and you'd join in, always knowing exactly what those men in suits were about to say, as they yelled as loudly as our neighbour Ŀiela. And one day, I heard you say that *tal-Għawdxija*, the folks who lived across the street, had hung lemons on their front door and you were minded to go pick those lemons and serve them up with a fish dinner just to get your own back, only your wife, who was a saint, put a stop to that. That day, as you lay there, I could finally read your party membership card stamped on your closed eyelids. And only then did I begin to understand who 'they' and 'the others' were.

One in the eye for you, then, Mifsud. But when you accosted the almighty in the village square and he smiled and tried to soothe you – 'You know, there must have been some kind of mistake, Mifsud. We wouldn't harm the Workers, now would we?' – you still had to say your piece. You took your rifle and bayonet along, remembering the hail of bullets as you sprawled against the A/A cannon and spat in the face of the Fascists and didn't even think about saving your own skin, and you said your piece to the almighty, told him what his lot had done to you. Little you, swinging this way and that on your bad leg, how dare you cut a furrow through that throng of thugs to speak to god almighty?

Pa, where are you going?

Shut up, you. Wait for me here and don't move.

But where are you going, Pa?

Nowhere. Just wait here and don't move.

But where are you going, Pa?

I'm going to have a word with that chap over there.

And I saw a mob standing around a type with a dirty look that I'd seen before, shouting on the telly, his mug plastered all over the walls in our streets. And I watched as you limped towards him, brushed those giants aside and spoke, earnestly shaking your head. And then you came back for me and we went home to eat our macaroni. And on Monday you brought your medal home: Mifsud, there was a mistake, you know. It wasn't you we meant to transfer. Starting tomorrow, you'll be reporting for work somewhere else. Somewhere closer to home, given your handicap, you poor man, you. We want nothing but the best for the Workers.

How could you not be afraid?

I don't want you to be afraid, understand? You're acting like a baby. And I don't want to see you cry over nothing. A wimp, that's what you are. Big boy like you, you should be scaring everyone off.

And I bite my lower lip, trying to hold back the tears.

Don't you have any guts? Don't you have any guts? You should make your way over there and knock them down, every last one of them. Don't let me see you cry again, you're not a baby anymore. Understand?

I take long, slow breaths. It's true, I'm not a baby. I'm tall and broad. I'm not a little girl. I'm the son, the son of the soldier who got the medals, who is afraid of nobody, not even the minister. I'm strong. One punch and I'd smash their teeth in, make their noses bleed, make them cry, break them, tear them apart.

Don't you have any guts? If I was built like you I'd knock them down, every last one of them. I'm telling you, I don't want to see you cry.

But I break down and cry. I cry because I've lost again. And I realise that my ultimate battle isn't against Barbara's gang, or against Franky, but against you. And I don't want to fight you because I … So I sit in the corner, or go up to the roof of the house, or out in the yard or the street, and cry. And as I cry I see you, with that heavy Humphrey Bogart stare, I see you stiff as a poker in your brown uniform, I see you with your bayonet, the shining medals on your chest, the helmet fastened around your chin, I see you sprawling against the white hot cannon aiming for the Stuka, I see you shooting for all you're worth and cursing the fascist bastards and the swastika, I see you speeding on a military motorbike that's twice your size, I see you soaked with rivulets of sweat, I see you roll up the sleeves of your uniform to expose the green tattoos across both arms because you're in the army, I see you and you tower to the skies, gigantic, a column of granite, a mountain, a lightning god.

In the name of the Father.

These images that I still carry with me. Like the time you caught me crying on the church parvis and you came up to me to ask what had happened. And I cursed you inwardly because you'd caught me one more time. And one more time I had to listen to your sermon, to you telling me that I should knock them all down, every last one of them. And to make me even more bitter, you went up to them and told them I was strong enough to knock them down, every last one of them. And I caught them laughing at you behind your back as you turned back to me with your soldier's glare. Tell me, what did you think of me when you saw me cry? Did I disappoint you? Did I make you lose it? Did I exasperate you because I was afraid of the dark? You know, I'm still afraid of the dark. Did you know that? Do you know that I still cry whenever I remember your wife, whenever I see her again, skeletal, gasping for breath? Do you know that I still cry whenever I find myself alone with your photographs, especially the one you took in Tel-El Kebir, in Egypt in March 1951? Or when I remember the story you told me about the aeroplane, the aeroplane that crashed with your mates on board, the ones you'd gone there to replace, the aeroplane that you yourself had boarded on its previous flight. Do you know that I've broken all your commandments? Do you know where I used to hang out while you thought I was at school or in the village square, or at mass, or sleeping in the room upstairs? What do you know about me? Do you know what messes I've found myself in, such messes as you wouldn't believe your cry-baby of a son could ever even dream of? Do you know? Of course you don't. With you, under your direction, I played a lengthy part. You were the director, I was the main actor. And I played that part so well that you could just sit there without moving and watch the drama unfold. And I'm so used to playing the role by now; I'll carry on, even though I'm tired, I'll carry on because I know the score, the script.

More footage from the archives. At the very back of the cupboard which harbours my memories, there's a short film that was shot one

Sunday afternoon. Ħal Far or Ta' Qali. Winter sunlight. You'd bought me a ball from Spiru. A colourful ball, with pictures of ducks or bears or whatever. We're standing perhaps three metres apart. And it's windy and there's the occasional strong gust. You shift your weight onto your bad leg and kick the ball with the other one, slowly, just enough for it to roll towards me. I dream a dream every time I kick the ball: when I grow up, I'll wear a white and black gear and play with the first eleven; when I grow up, I'll join the national football team; when I grow up, I'll have a decent pair of football boots, with proper studs; when I grow up I won't run after the ball in canvas shoes with banana-shaped studs. I'll wear proper Adidas gear and Superga shoes like Jason's got. But no, this story can't be right. That Sunday in Ħal Far or Ta' Qali must have happened well before these dreams began. Three metres apart and the wind blowing from all sides. You shift your weight onto your bad leg and shoot the ball, slowly, just enough for it to roll towards me. I'm not lame like you, I don't need to shift my weight onto one leg. So I take a deep breath and give the ball the strongest kick I've ever given in my life. Your leg's just not up to it and the ball goes right past you and on its way. It was a cheap ball, easily carried by the wind. And I see you going after the ball as fast as you can and the wind blowing stronger and stronger and the ball getting further and further away; so far away that you're just a speck in the distance, unrecognisable but for your swinging gait. And then I see you from far away, coming back slowly and I begin to tremble because I feel guilty for the first time in my life. And I pity you. I pity you so much I could cry. This is probably the first memory I have of you. I can't have been older than four on that Sunday that I can't forget. Look at the poor man, look how far he's had to walk to get the ball. It's all my fault, I kicked it too hard. My poor father plays ball with me in spite of his limp and what do I go and do? I kick it over to the other side. My poor father. From that day onwards, I always looked upon you with pity, the same pity that I felt for you in the Upper Savoy cinema on the day I turned sixteen.

And I suddenly realise that it all comes back to the Name of the Father: the first memories of you, the first bouts of tears, the first battles, the first tensions. All in the Name of the Father. This big, potent phallus that rears its head out of the murky depths that surround me. There are so many things I wanted to tell you about myself but never did. There were so many times when I wanted to tell you who I am but kept myself in check. I wanted to tell you how, in my middle age, I made a son more complicated than you could possibly imagine. As I struggled to snatch your wife away from you I fixed my gaze upon your image to make sure I knew the enemy, the rival in this battle that I thought would never end. How could I struggle against a soldier with three stripes and a chest hung with medals? How could I use my sling when you were shooting a cannon? We were like David and Goliath. Or Abraham and Isaac. And then one day the skies above me opened up and I heard this thundering voice say that it was well pleased in me. And I looked up and wanted to cry because, as you know very well, of all Man's gestures, crying is the most sublime. You taught me that, when I saw you cry in the stillness of the Addolorata cemetery.

My own hands have stained, but only with ink, ink as black as soot, as black as the mourning band I had already prepared in memory of you, one week after I was born and had begun to recognise you as you looked at me with eyes that passed no judgement.

Shall I then, like you, begin to crush beneath my heel the scented flowers, while singing a paean to the roses of May?

What does it mean, this vapid stare, this whiteness clouding over, this pupil's empty husk? Tell me, what verses should I read now, pervaded as we are by this long silence? *Here's the first lesson you should memorise for life: I am your father, I made you without wanting you. And here's the second, following on the first: I'd give my life for you, my son, because your flesh is of my flesh, your blood is of my blood: were it not for me, you'd not exist.* And I look at you today and am well pleased in you. I remember you in November 1991, as I descended, degree certificate in hand, and there you were, the son of Pawla and Salvatore Mifsud, orphaned at a young age, a nameless proletarian, soldier, unskilled worker, there you were with your wife, your faces all lit up. That boy, everything scared him, he'd cry for no good reason, but there he was now, wearing a toga and yes, you were so pleased that maybe you'd forgotten how angry you'd become whenever tears would well up in his eyes.

There's something I would have liked to tell you, after the nurse came to help me carry you: I would have liked the palms of my hands to become stained like yours. Instead, I set myself adrift, lulled by the water.

See now: my hands aren't marked like yours, although the skin is somewhat wrinkled. It's wrinkled from caressing this coarse flesh, riddled with cracks, ravaged by years, brimming with love. I forgot to attend to your words. The scent of myrrh and aloe is overpowering and the smell of cinnamon goes to the head. All right then, I didn't forget, I wanted to touch the apple's core and taste it for myself. Did you not taste the fruit of smiling Eve? Didn't you? Didn't you? That day, she embraced me and kissed me, looking straight into my eyes. And as she took off all her clothes she told me in a whisper: today I've paid my vows. Therefore I came forth to seek you, to meet you, to find you.

And I was ready.

Square

Towards the end of February, the sun shone bright. You were walking ahead of us. On sand littered with algae and dead twigs. The bay was strewn with dead jellyfish. I saw you spear a fat one on the end of a stick and carry it over dangling on the tip to show it to me. I said yeuch and you smiled. Something of a rarity, that – your smiling. As always, your face was half concealed behind dark glasses. As always, your head was bowed. You're always looking downwards. You never raise your head. As usual, you walked with an odd gait: as though you were swinging, as though you walked on springs, as though you were … lame. You know, you walk a little oddly, papinku. Me, I don't. I run all over the place, picking up stones and throwing them into the sea. I taunt the sea with stones. Stone after stone. Pebbles that have come up for a rest from the currents at Golden Bay. And then you sit down on a little rock. You're always sitting down. Maminka takes out my spade and plastic bucket and kneels on the sand beside me, digging it up while I shovel it into the bucket. And you sit there all the while, alone. Not with us. Alone. I want to build a big sand castle. I want to build a really big one. So I pack the sand into the bucket with my green and yellow spade. And you call out to me because you want to take a picture, but I've got a castle to build, I've no time for pictures. You take your pictures. One after the other. I want to build a sand castle so that I can enjoy tearing it down. Then, just as I'm finishing the castle, you get up and walk away. Alone. Not far from where the foam boldly laps the shoreline. You call me and I come next to you and with a dead twig in your hand you etch a square in the wet sand littered with lifeless jellyfish. Look at the square, you say. Now we'll wait for the sea to come closer. And the sea does come closer and when it ebbs away I realise that the square has disappeared. And you etch another square and up comes the foam to take it away. Where's the square? you ask. The sea took it away. There, look, there it is in the sea. And you smile and with your head bowed towards the ground you try to find the square that the foam has dragged away. Once upon a time there was a square and the sea got close to it and it disappeared. But I want a square that won't go away and so I ask for your twig and you give it to me promptly and I promptly throw it into the water and watch as it too disappears. I see my mother smiling and I forget all about the disappearing squares and the twig. And I run over to her. She looks so beautiful in the sunlight, surrounded by sand, her fingers covered with it, her loose hair like a swing.

Tell me, my son, what memories does your mind dredge up? Which early image has left its mark? Which one is the foundation on which all other images were built? My own is sad, so very sad. And yours? Do you remember the singing, softly whispered, in the half dark of nights interrupted by hunger and by tears? Or the cloth rattle in the shape of a little bear? Or those colourful butterflies above your head, spinning in time to music while you stared wide-eyed and tried to understand? Do you remember staring at me tongue-tied in the car as I sang to you about a twinkling star? Do you remember me staring amazed at you?

On the day when you announced your imminent arrival, we rushed to hospital with a bag full of the armour that was meant to protect you and another bag full of small bottles of water that we'd kept refrigerated for about a week. I wanted to witness your coming, to have your arrival stamped indelibly in the pupils of my eyes, wide open, bloodshot from a twelve-hour spell beneath the sterile neon light. June. It was the feast of St Peter and St Paul, the day of the *Imnarja*. Not far off, fireworks stirred up the night, shattering the dark with bursts of colour. The midwife, her assistant, the blinding white light, the red digits blinking on the machine that measured blood pressure and heart rate, the heat, the sweat (welling up from the pores at first, then dripping, then trickling down, then gushing), blood and water, and then you, what little hair you had slicked back with blood and goo. And your complaint, your first, arrived on the back of a sneeze. You hardly cried. Actually, we caught you smiling in the first picture we took of you. That was the first look you ever gave me: your eyes so serious, your lips smiling. Lying exhausted between your mother's bloody legs, you decided to begin to wail. Go on and wail. This is just the beginning. That's your mother there, surrounded by machines blinking with numbers, looking at you. That's your mother. Me, I'm your father. I saw you the first time some months ago. An oddly-shaped soundscape printed on a photograph.

Then the midwife hands me a pair of scissors. I cut you loose from your mother. I hack through your sole point of contact. I separate you. I release you. I bear the phallus. And here I am, already interfering. Cutting you loose. Hacking through you. The void that yawns before you must be filled. Scissors in hand I look at you again, drowsy, tired, shocked. You want to cry, you want to sleep, you want to suckle, you want to rest against the breast to hear the beat that kept you company, which you can only catch from a distance now. You want to get over the shock but you're still trembling. Don't be afraid of me, in spite of this sharp pointed instrument in my hand. They did this to me as well. And now it's my turn. I look at you – drowsy, tired, shocked – and raise the scissors, half expecting the angel's command to stay my hand and spare my son. I try to catch a glimpse of the goat caught by its horns in the thicket. The red digits blink, the nurse works on the sutures, the midwife urging me on. The sweat and goo, the blood, the tangled cord. *Come on, come on, do it.*

And I approach, reluctant. You are stunned.

Stabat Mater

Julia Kristeva with her son.[5] The smell of milk, of dewed greenery. Her newborn son dancing in her neck, fluttering at her hair, seeking a bare shoulder, descending towards her breast. On her navel, he dreams the dream. Kristeva sighs, 'My son.' Throughout the sleepless, interrupted nights, this warm mercury in her arms; carresses, affection, this defenceless body – hers, his – sheltered, protected.

Stabat Mater.

It all comes back to her, to Julia: her mother's bed, her mother, the exit, the retreat. This very bed. These very sheets: alone: she, I and he.

She, I and he.

In the adjoining room, the midwife, I and he. The midwife rushes ahead to weigh this human being. Prone on the scales, in this room as white as death, it was just us: she, I and he. He: staring wide-eyed, yawning, grimacing, trembling from the shock, searching for the cord that wasn't there. I: looking at this human being weighed. I look at him looking at me. In this white, deathly as death. As dead as her. As she. As my own mother wandering in, white as blood that's ebbed away, as a heart with clogged arteries, chemical white, white as the sheets drenched with the water from her calves, white as the smell of medication.

In the room, it was just us: she, I and he. The languor of this brand-new body on the scales reminds me of the deathly languor of my mother.

---

[5] Kristeva, Julia (1987) 'Stabat Mater', *Tales of Love*, New York: Columbia University Press

Alone: she, I and he.

And I was afraid.

And I took you back into my arms and felt the spasm of the void. The unbearable lightness of being. The unparalleled lightness of the body. I remember: in bed, with her: that pleasure so opaque, as Kristeva calls it, that it anchors me to the sheets. I walk with you in my arms to put you on the breast that's laid for you, so that you'll hear the heart, taste the milk, sleep deeply, sleep your tremors off.

Stabat pater.

Like Kristeva, I realise that your face is already human, already you have the wordless gift of speech. And I am filled with emptiness.

I call with the news. The first time I make the announcement, my voice begins to falter, my legs are unsteady. I look straight out of the window, closed in spite of the tremendous heat. The light of night and the silence that probably reigns out there. *Hello. Hello. Is that Manuel? Is everything alright? Is everything alright? How did it go?* But my voice is faltering and there's a lump in my throat that's preventing me from speaking. And the tears start to fall, a lot of tears. As I look out at the void in this solitary moment, I see me lurking in the blackness of the windowpane.

Tremens factus sum ego, et timeo ...

I get home at three in the morning. Alone. My clothes are soaked. In the silence and the darkness, a cold wetness against my skin, a warm wetness in my eyes. As I rinse myself of the day I discover that my arms are still in the same position. The images dissolve into sleep, on the bed where the whole story began: yours and mine.

What now?

The day I touched you you were trembling still. We were both trembling. We were wary of each other. That was our first time. The first time I saw you unclothed and touched you. Believe me, of all the naked bodies I have touched, yours was the most beautiful. How many times have my fingers touched another's nakedness, how many times have I been overwhelmed by the body's lust for flesh. That lightness, the empty space that somehow filled my arms. Fearfully, I touched you and took you into my arms: your wrinkled body, that eloquent, wordless look. Perhaps these words shouldn't be said. After all, I didn't carry you within me, though I'd have liked to.[6] A man, I cannot feel this frailty emerging, hard, from within me. I didn't lay myself bare to finally bear you, exhausted. Water.

Early in the morning in the office with the country's flag, the woman in lipstick and Versace glasses asks me to give you a name. Nikol Matej Mifsud. Today, the Republic of Malta officially welcomes Nikol Matej Mifsud as one of its citizens and hereby bestows upon him a number, the brand of the state. Today, the Republic of Malta recognises you as a political animal and hereby considers you its offspring, a member of the inner circle, and solemnly swears to do its utmost to protect, nurture and sustain you.

In the Name of the Father, according to Jacques Lacan.[7]

In the Name of the Father who made you.

In the Name of the Father who took your mother for his own.

Your mother is not yours, son, although she is your mother – the mother of you.

Your mother is not yours, son, although she was your home – the home of you. That is where you began – inside her, inside she who is

---

[6] Yes, I would have liked to. I'm a man after all. No doubt, as Cixous would promptly remind me: 'It is the men who like to play with dolls. As we've known ever since Pygmalion. Their old dream: to be God the mother. The best mother, the second one, the one who gives the second birth.' Cixous, Hélène (1977) 'La Jeune Née', *Diacritics* 7(2)

[7] Lacan, Jacques (1966) *Écrits*, Éditions Seuil

your mother, the mother of you. You nurtured yourself on her system as you formed your own. It was just you two together: you and she. Alone. Alone together. And then the midwife handed me a pair of scissors and I severed the tie that bound you once and for all. Don't be angry: I too must play a part in this story. Don't be shocked that I was there before you; my own father was there before me. I know what it means, that look you give me as you embrace her. I gave that look myself before you did, to a man you've never met, though you've seen his lifeless, vapid stare a couple of times. It's no longer just the two of you now, you've become three. We've become three: you, she and I. I know what it means, that look you give me. I gave that look myself before you did. I gave that look when I too imagined the phallus.

There is the Name of the Father, son. When I watch you sitting on the floor, I'm fascinated by your strength. You hold yourself as upright as a peg driven into the ground. You hit the floor and reach out for your doll. I'm fascinated by the poetry you mutter. I'm fascinated by your solitary laughter. I'm fascinated when I see you off on your way to nursery school. I smile ruefully when you wail because I came to pick you up instead of her. You wail because you think she's abandoned you. You wail because you think I'm worth more to her than you. You wail because you feel overcome by the weight of the Name of the Father pressing down on you. I know what it means, your insistence to be with the two of us all the time. I recognise the tone with which you order me to go into my room, to disappear, leaving you to enjoy what I myself had claimed. I won't give in to you, because that's the Law of the Father.

In the evening, before bed, you hug your mother, kiss her for a long time, hug her again one last time, then kiss her again. And you drink your milk from the blue cup with the smiling yellow bear. *Tell me a story.*

Once upon a time there was a little boy named Plumpton. Plumpton lived under a big red mushroom with white spots. But one day, the big bad wolf came along. He tore up the mushroom and took it away. Plumpton was so sad! He cried and cried until the beautiful fairy came along and said, 'Plumpton, why are you crying?' And Plumpton replied, 'Because the big bad wolf came along and took away my mushroom and now I have nowhere to live.' The beautiful fairy gave Plumpton a big hug and said, 'Don't worry, we'll find you another mushroom. Let me call the yellow bird, because he can fly high and spot where the mushrooms are.' So the yellow bird came and Plumpton got onto his back and off they flew. They flew very very far and very very high. Finally, they flew over a big forest with lots of trees and suddenly, the yellow bird spotted a big mushroom and put Plumpton down next to it. Plumpton was so happy! He told the yellow bird, 'Thank you very much, yellow bird. Now I've got a place to live.' The yellow bird smiled and flew off. And Plumpton kept on looking at him until he couldn't see him anymore. Then Plumpton lay down beneath the mushroom and slept.

In the forest where we spend our holidays every winter, wrapped in jackets with hoods over our heads, our hands buried in gloves, we search for mushrooms so that, should the big bad wolf turn up again and take Plumpton's home away, we'll have a new one ready. Suddenly, a fistful of snow falls off a branch and frightens you and you ask me whether it's the big bad wolf, loitering somewhere close by. Could be. The big bad wolf is very bad indeed. But don't be afraid, I'm here and I'm holding your hand. Let's look for a mushroom for Plumpton. Then we hear a sound coming from the treetops and you're frightened again. Don't be afraid, that's probably the yellow bird looking for a mushroom, just like we are. Come on, let's beat him to it! And so we walk through the snow and there, beneath a very big tree, we spot a brown mushroom calling out to us, and your face lights up and you forget all about the big bad wolf prowling just a few metres away and off you go to pick the mushroom. But before we pick it, I take a picture of you next to it, as a souvenir. And we take the frozen mushroom home. But now we need to find out where Plumpton is. So we put the mushroom in a bag on the windowsill. And we wait for him, while we watch the snow falling, coating the coated ground. We wait and wait, until it's dark and we both begin to doze off.

And then during the night, when everyone's dreaming of snowmen and deer who have lost their way, Plumpton climbs up the windows to reach the mushroom and next morning, it's nowhere to be found.

If tomorrow you were to echo Sylvia Plath and say to me that you've had to kill me, you'd only remind me that I've done the same. I killed my father many times, in many ways. I killed him when, as a young child, I put on the black band that presaged my mourning. I killed him the day I kicked the ball with all my strength and it was borne away by the wind and by the time he'd snatched it and brought it back to me, I had exhausted him. I killed him the day I decided that my father wasn't my father, that there must be another man, hidden somewhere, who was my real father, that my father was Joseph: a little cog in a very big wheel. I killed him when I decided I wouldn't walk in the shadow of the Name of the Father. I killed him when I took the tablets inscribed with his commandments and having let them slip out of my grasp, I trampled on the broken fragments. I killed him when I became, not a man, but something else.

If tomorrow, you were to say,

> *Well, son, what can I say, except that maybe you're right? I did kill you, didn't I? I killed you the day I followed the midwife's orders, the day I took the woman you loved away from you, the day I hung around your neck an amulet with my face on it, under whose weight you staggered. Daddy, daddy, you bastard, I'm through.*[8]

---

[8] Plath, Sylvia (1965) 'Daddy', *Ariel*, London: Faber & Faber

Father/Son Authority, Privilege, Strength[9]

Well, son, what can I say, except that maybe you're right? Do you know that it's morning already? And soon enough you'll be up and running about and hollering and pulling out all your toys while my eyes are a fiery red, red-rimmed with sleep. I've been up all night: I was writing a story for you and I wanted to hang it up on the headboard over your bed but on my way there I just dozed off. I'm tired of playing the part of the almighty. In the middle of the night, when the rooster in the garden behind our place was already up, I had to give in. My head aches, my eyes feel like rocks, and I don't know if I can make it through the day. But do go on and make your plans. That's what I did myself, one day.

You're like a baby. Your hands are cold. Lying on your side, with your head buried in the blankets. You're almost invisible. And you look as though you'd shrunk. Your eyes are lost in a sea of wrinkles; lost in the void, in the dark, in the moment that we've been expecting for a long time. They look but do not see or see nothing but blur. I approach you: Pa, how are you? Can you hear me? It's Manuel. I've come to see you. I'm going to stay here by your side, ok? How do you feel? My brothers and sisters were here but now I've arrived and I'll stay here by your side, alright? Can you recognise me? It's Manuel. Are you thirsty? Do you want some water?

I've no idea whether he was conscious or not. The nurse told me that in the state he was in, he could still hear everything and she gave me a warning sign to be careful what I said. I sat there pointlessly, looking at my infant boy. He is so small, so fragile, so vulnerable. I wish I could hold him in my arms and hug him to me. This scene is familiar. Years before, I was sitting next to another bed that resembled this one. There were tubes, uncertain whether to carry on pumping chemicals or just give up. There was the bald woman in the next bed

---

[9] Cixous, Hélène (1977) 'La Jeune Nee', *Diacritics* 7(2)

who'd been admitted on her feet and had sunk into a bottomless coma. There were other hearts getting ready to cease. There were many clogged arteries, many attacks in the middle of the night, many silences, many sadnesses. This is all too familiar. Every twenty minutes or so, this infant boy opens his eyes, rolls them and closes them again. Every twenty minutes I get up from my chair and stand close to him, smiling at him, caressing his cold forehead and talking to him. And then I sit down again. I don't know whether I should carry on talking to him or not. Perhaps he's making one last effort to talk to me, perhaps it's an effort he could expend on something more worthwhile. I suddenly feel the urge to sing to him:

> *Underneath the lantern*
> *By the barrack gate,*
> *Darling I remember*
> *The way you used to wait.*
> *T'was there that you whispered tenderly*
> *That you loved me;*
> *You'd always be*
> *My Lili of the lamplight,*
> *Wie einst Lili Marlene,*
> *Wie einst Lili Marlene.*

Once again, I find that my voice has deserted me. I feel like crying. I feel like retreating into a corner to watch everything unfold from a distance. I feel like staying here to watch the hero's final act. The languor in this whiteness reminds me of that corner next to labour room 7. It reminds me of that eloquent, wordless look. It reminds me of the emptiness, the unbearable lightness of the being that comes to an end. It reminds me that life is only to be found elsewhere, not here. *La vraie est absent.*[10]

---

[10] Rimbaud, Arthur 'Vierge Folle: L'époux infernal'

The phone. Manuel, you'd better come.

This sentence too is familiar. I heard it many years before, one night at about two thirty in the morning as I watched Sonny and Cher shaking their heads like dolls and singing *I Got You Babe*.

Should I bring your rifle along with me? Should I decorate your chest with the medals hanging in a frame in the living room where I sat waiting for the phone to ring? Should I prepare myself to tell you the things I've never said?

It's almost as if you'd agreed between yourselves to have your funerals on special days. Mater on Christmas Eve; Pater on Labour Day. The proletarian who was never an aristocrat because he had the wrong party membership card had to be buried on the day that was once dedicated to him.

But this is not the last of my memories.

Two years later:

At the Addolorata cemetery. A beautiful day in May. Three gravediggers uproot the black marble slab. One of them goes 'down there' and begins to bring up the junk: skeletons and mildewed coffins, cardboard moist with damp. The one down below shouts up to the ones above: 'Man coming up first. It's a man, Karm.' And the one above replies: 'OK, send it up! Is there anything left down there?' And the man below replies: 'A woman. I'm sending her up, Karm.' Then, the one who remained above, together with the third man, spreads everything out on the ground. The woman was buried wearing a blue dress. 'Will you just look at that,' says the third man who's said nothing so far, 'that dress is as good as new. You could take it away with you if you wanted. And that's the man, see, in jacket and tie.' As he rummages about, an identity card slips out of the jacket pocket. 'You'll want to take this, yeah? Here you go, who's going to take it? Now we'll just pack the rest up in boxes. You got the boxes, right? Good. What shall we do with that dress? I say we throw it away. We should throw his clothes away too.' Then the woman is stripped and her remains are quickly gathered and packed into the first box. Then the chief gravedigger shouts at the other, 'Watch it. Careful. Lift him by the jacket and pull him out, come on. And bring the clothes over here so we can throw them away.' And then the other man grabs the jacket by the shoulders, and the contents fall through and crash to the ground. 'Fuckin' idiot, I said watch it!' As they crash to the ground, some of the bones splinter. And then, the Headman's head begins to roll down the hill until it hits the edge of the tomb and stops and fixes me with a stare.

And that's the last wordless, eloquent look you gave me, father. A few seconds, no more, because then the chief came along and grabbed your skull by the eye sockets and threw it onto the pile in the second box, pressed it all down and snapped the lid shut. And while the other two lowered the boxes down and sealed the slabs shut and laid down the marble slab, the chief sidled up and I slipped him a twenty and told him to have a drink on me, but he quickly informed me that when they bring up two, their palms have to be greased a bit more. And so I slipped him another twenty. 'God rest the souls of those we've just brought up, Mister.'

And that's the final image. The hero's absolute demise.

Now, carry on looking at the sea while I rest my curving spine. Keep looking in the distance and hold on to that sand bucket because look, the waves are rolling in once more and you could gather the entire sea into that bucket. Then walk along the bay with the blue sea in your bucket and pick the cockle shells and gather the sand. Throw it all into the bucket. Leave the dead jellyfish behind: you have no use for rubbish. When you've gathered all the sand, walk along the road and uproot every tree you find, and shove them all into the bucket, one by one. Walk on. When you reach the other end, stop, sit down and rest.

By the time you get there, a new sun will have risen. The wolf will probably be lost among the snow-laden trees. And Plumpton will have built a house of bricks that can withstand the wind, he'll have moved in, grown up and died. Sit down and close your eyes and if your tears start to fall just let the wind dry them for you. And if you hear the music, sing along.

Afterword

About seven weeks after Maria Handke committed suicide at the age of fifty-one, her son Peter began to write a memoir of his mother, *Wunschloses Unglück*. Towards the end of the book, Peter Handke writes: 'It is not true that writing has helped me. In my weeks of preoccupation with the story, the story has not ceased to preoccupy me.' And he continues: 'Sometimes, of course, as I worked on my story, my frankness and honesty weighed on me and I longed to write something that would allow me to lie and dissemble a bit ...'

Now that the last sentence has been written and I've turned the page and found the cover, I can finally take a deep breath and turn out the light.

Notes

The following are brief descriptions of some persons, places and traditions mentioned in the text.

Biskuttin

A small, sweet biscuit. Traditionally, this was one of the items served during wedding celebrations and christenings. The phrase *jiekol il-biskuttin* ('to eat a biskuttin') is sometimes used idiomatically to imply that one is getting married or is about to have a child.

l-Imnarja

The feast of St. Peter and St. Paul on the 29th of June and one of the oldest folk festivals celebrated in Malta. The word is a corruption of the Italian *Luminara* and literally means 'festival of light', after the bonfires that were lit on the occasion. The feast is today mostly celebrated around the area of Buskett, rabbit being one of the traditional dishes served on the occasion.

Ellul Mercer, Ġużè (1897 – 1961)

Politician, journalist and prolific writer. Ellul Mercer joined the Labour Party in 1924 and was a member of the National Assembly that drafted a new Constitution for Malta in 1947. He was three times elected to the House of Representatives. As a writer, he is often considered a key figure in the development of realism in Maltese prose and is best known for his 1935 novel *Leli ta' Ħaż-Żgħir* and *Taħt in-Nar* ('Under Fire'), a diary of the first year of World War II published in 1949.

Grima, Joseph (b. 1936)

Politician and broadcaster. After an early career as a radio broadcaster, first in the Rediffusion Company and then in the Malta Broadcasting Authority, Grima contested the 1976 general elections with the Labour Party and became a member of parliament after a casual election. For the next five years, he served as Dominic Montoff's special envoy to several countries in Europe, North Africa and the Middle East. Grima was re-elected in 1981 and served first as minister of industry and then of tourism. Following his retirement from politics in 1992, Grima became increasingly involved in radio and television broadcasting, having established his own radio station in 1991. Following an arson attack on the station in 1998, he joined NET TV, a station owned by the Nationalist Party. He currently presents a program on One TV, which is part of the Labour Party's media network.

Marsa

A heavily industrialised town in the South-East of Malta, in the Harbour area. In the period evoked in this book Marsa, like other urban areas in the South, would have been viewed as primarily working-class.

Moran, Vincent (b. 1932)

Politician. A doctor by profession, Moran joined the Labour Party in 1948 and was elected to parliament seven times between 1962 and 1992, before resigning from the Labour parliamentary group in 1995. He served as minister of health and the environment in the 1976 and 1981 legislatures and was responsible for the introduction of the national health scheme in Malta.

Sant, Lorry (1937 – 1995)

Politician. Sant's early political involvement was as an activist with the Labour League of Youth and later in the General Workers' Union. He was elected for the first time in 1962 and successfully contested five subsequent elections. During the 1970s and 1980s, his portfolio included various ministries, notably the ministry of works and the ministry of the interior. Sant was suspended from all Labour Party activities in 1990. He remains a controversial figure, whose name has been associated with corruption and violence during the 1980s.

Wall, The

The film in question is *Pink Floyd: The Wall* (1982; dir: Alan Parker) based on the album released by Pink Floyd in 1979.

Xgħajra Tower

Xgħajra is a village in the South-East of Malta. The tower referenced here is one of thirteen watchtowers erected by the Knights of Malta under the reign of Grandmaster de Redin between 1658 and 1659.

About the author

Immanuel Mifsud was born in Malta in 1967. He has published several volumes of short stories and poems and was the winner of the 2002 Malta National Book Award for Prose. He has also published short stories for children and a collection of lullabies in Maltese. In 2011 he published the first volume in a series of collections of fairy tales from various European countries.

In the Name of the Father (and of the Son) was awarded the European Union Prize for Literature in 2011.

Parthian Books: Recommended Fiction

The Blue Tent
Richard Gwyn
ISBN 978-1-912681-28-0
£9.99 Paperback

'One of the most satisfying, engrossing and
perfectly realised novels of the year.'
– *The Western Mail*

"This book is itself a sort of portal, where the
novelist-as-alchemist builds us a house
in the hills and then fills it ... with a
convincing magic.'
– *Nation.Cymru*

'A mysterious, dream-like story, delicately-
written and with a disturbing undertow,
The Blue Tent is in the best tradition of
modern oneiric fiction.'
– Patrick McGuinness

The Levels
Helen Pendry
ISBN 978-1-912109-40-1
£8.99 Paperback

'...with all the tension and plot twists and
turns that you would expect from a gripping
crime novel, makes an unsettling,
compelling read.'
– *Morning Star*

'...this is an assured novel and marks Helen
Pendry as an important new literary voice.'
– Kirsti Bohata, *Wales Arts Review*

'This is an elegant, wise and warm story that
stays with you long after finishing it.'
– Mike Parker

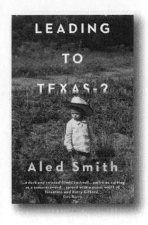

Leading to Texas-2
Aled Smith
ISBN 978-1-912109-11-1
£8.99 Paperback

'Aled Smith has mixed a dark and
twisted filmic cocktail.'
– Des Barry

Zero Hours on the Boulevard
ed. Alexandra Büchler
& Alison Evans
ISBN 978-1-912109-12-8
£8.99 Paperback

'A book about friendship, community,
identity and tribalism...'
– *New Welsh Reader*

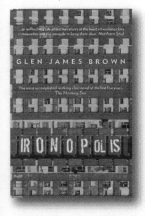

Ironopolis
Glen James Brown
ISBN 978-1-912681-09-9
£9.99 Paperback

'The most accomplished working-class
novel of the last few years.'
– *Morning Star*

'...nothing short of a triumph.'
– *The Guardian*

Parthian Fiction

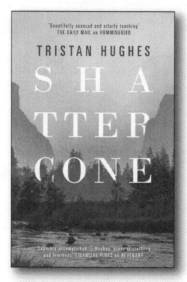

SHATTERCONE
Tristan Hughes
978-1-912681-47-1
£10.00

**HELLO FRIEND WE
MISSED YOU**
Richard Owain Roberts
978-1-912681-49-5
£11.99

PARTHIAN

PARTHIAN

CARNIVALE

2 0 1 9 / 21

La Blanche
Maï-Do Hamisultane
Translated by Suzy Ceulan Hughes
ISBN 978-1-91-268123-5
£8.99 • Paperback

TRANSLATED BY JULIA AND PETER SHERWOOD

The Night Circus
and Other Stories
Uršuľa Kovalyk

TRANSLATED BY SUZY CEULAN HUGHES

La Blanche
Maï-Do Hamisultane

The Night Circus
and Other Stories
Uršuľa Kovalyk
Translated by Julia and
Peter Sherwood
ISBN 978-1-91-268104-4
£8.99 • Paperback

Fiction in Translation

The Book of Katerina
Auguste Corteau
Translated by Claire Papamichael
ISBN 978-1-91-268126-6
£8.99 • Paperback

TRANSLATED BY CLAIRE PAPAMICHAEL

The Book of Katerina
Auguste Corteau

'Filled with magical worth, therapeutic, artistic... and playful. Playful about
the woman who writes, about the woman who suffers...'
MIREN IBARLUZEA, BIZKAIE

A Glass Eye
Miren Agur Meabe

A Glass Eye
Miren Agur Meabe
Translated by Amaia Gabantxo
ISBN 978-1-91-210954-8
£8.99 • Paperback

Her Mother's Hands
Karmele Jaio
Translated by Kristin Addis
ISBN 978-1-91-210955-5
£8.99 • Paperback

WINNER
ENGLISH PEN
AWARD

WINNER
Euskadi Prize Prize

WINNER
Zazpi Kale Prize

Seventh Igartza
Prize

'Jaio is undoubtedly a very skilful narrator'
IÑIGO ROQUE, GARA

Her Mother's Hands
Karmele Jaio

PARTHIAN
CARNIVALE
2 0 1 9 / 2 1